MOUSE TALES

Story by
Philip Roy

Art by
Andrea Torrey Balsara

RONSDALE PRESS

"John?"

"*Mmmf!* . . . What?"

"I can't sleep."

"Oh."

"Will you tell me a bedtime story?"

"A bedtime story?"

"Yes. Because if you tell me a story, I will be asleep even before you finish it. That's what happens."

"Well, I could tell you the story of Hansel and Gretel. But you might find it a little scary because it has a witch in it."

"John. Don't be silly. It's only a story, so how can I be afraid? Besides, witches aren't even real, so how can I be afraid of them?"

"Okay. Let's see . . . Hansel and Gretel were two kids who were very poor."

"Like us?"

"Even more poor than us."

"How poor were they?"

"So poor, their father couldn't even keep them anymore, so he gave them a piece of bread and sent them into the forest to live."

"That's TERRIBLE!"

"I know. But that's how poor they were."

"Anyway, the forest was dark and deep and kind of spooky."

"That's not scary."

"Yes, but there was a wicked witch who lived there."

"Oh."

"She lived in a gingerbread house that was decorated with candy."

"Candy?"

"Yes."

"She made her house out of GINGERBREAD and CANDY?"

"Yes."

"Well, she can't be THAT bad."

Welcome, Children

"She WAS that bad because she used the house to trick children, to catch them, and eat them."

"She ATE children?"

"Yes."

"Oh."

"I told you it was kind of scary."

"It's just a story, John, so it's not really scary. But we'd better warn Hansel and Gretel not to get too close to her house."

"It was too late. They found the house and started eating it."

"That's what I would do, too, but I would run away as soon as the witch came."

"Well, the witch saw them first and took them into her house."

"YIKES!
Did she eat them?"

"No. When she opened her oven, they pushed her in and ran away."

"Oh. Well, that's not too scary. Why do people even say witches are scary?"

"Probably because of how they look."

"What do they look like?"

"Umm . . . usually old and bent over, with long, crooked noses, and white hair, and a broom."

"A broom?"

"Yup. Witches ride brooms."

"In the air?"

"Yup."

"That sounds like fun."

"Are you sleepy yet, Happy?"

"Not yet. What else do witches do?"

"They cook magic stews in big pots and
keep spooky things in little jars."

"What kinds of things?"

"Things like . . . bat wings."

"That's not scary."

"Oh! Sorry, Happy. I wasn't thinking."

"John. Did you say . . . '*mice tails*?'"

"Yes, but . . ."

"In a jar?"

"Happy. It's only a story. Witches aren't real, remember?"

"I know. Okay. I think I'm ready to go to sleep now, John."

"Really?"

"Mmmhmm."

"Oh. Okay. Goodnight, Happy. Have a good sleep."

"Goodnight, John."

"John?"

"Yes?"

"How do the witches get the mice tails?"

"I don't know. I suppose they cut them off."

"Oh. Okay. Thanks. Goodnight, John."

"Goodnight, Happy."

"John?"

"Yes?"

"What do you think the witches cut the tails off with, a knife?"

"Probably. Maybe a hatchet."

"A hatchet?"

"It's like a small axe."

"Oh. Okay. Goodnight, John."

"Goodnight, Happy."

"John?"

"What?"

"We should make some warm milk and honey. It will help us fall asleep. We should get up, put all the lights on, sit at the kitchen table just like in the daytime, and have a nice cup of warm milk and honey. Don't you think that's a good idea?"

"I'm pretty tired, Happy. But I suppose we could warm some milk and honey."

"It will help us sleep, John. And we should turn all the lights on, too."

"Are you feeling a little scared, Happy?"

"Of course not. But I think I heard something."

"You heard something?"

"I think it was outside. You better check outside, John."

"Okay. I'll check. Nope. Nothing outside."

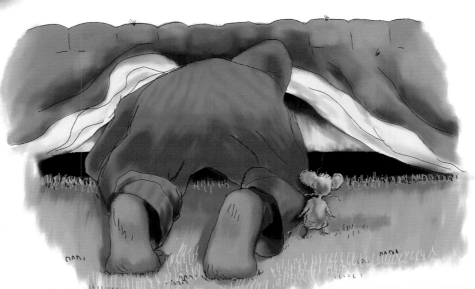

"Actually, I think it was coming from the bathroom. You better check in there."

"Okay. Nope. Nothing in there."

"Actually, I think it was coming from under the bed. You better check under the bed, John."

"Okay. Nope. Nothing under the bed."

"John?"

"Yes?"

"You know the old lady who lives downstairs?"

"Mrs. Farrell? Yes?"

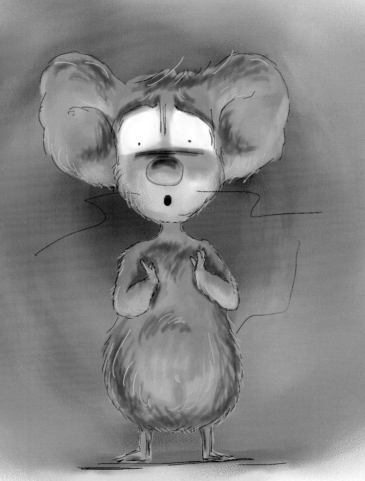

"I think she's a WITCH."

"WHAT? Oh, no, Happy. Mrs. Farrell is not a witch;
she's a sweet old lady."

"But she's old, John. And she's got white hair. And her nose is kind of long and crooked. I'm pretty sure she's a witch. What do you think we should do?"

"Happy. Lots of people are old and have white hair."

"But she has a broom, John. I've seen it."

"Happy, WE have a broom. That doesn't make us witches."

"But she makes magic stews. I smelled cooking outside her door. I bet she keeps things in little jars."

"I should have told you a different story, Happy.
    We'd be sleeping by now."

"I'm glad you told me about witches, John.
    Now I know what to look for."

"Happy. I'm so tired.
Do you think maybe you
    can go to sleep now?"

"Actually, John, now that all the lights are on, I was thinking,
                maybe we should clean
                    the apartment."

"Clean the apartment? It's the middle of the night! I'm sorry, but I'm too tired to do anything but sleep. You can stay up if you want to, but I'm going back to bed."

"You're going to go to sleep and leave me all alone?"

"You don't have to be alone. You can look at picture books."

"*Hmmmf!*"

(later)

"John . . . John! Wake up."

"*Whaa . . . t?*"

"I made you a coffee."

"What?"

"I made you a coffee. Now you can wake up."

"Happy, I didn't know you knew
how to make coffee."

"It's the easiest thing in the world.
You just put water in the kettle and pour it over
the coffee powder.
Then you put milk and sugar in."

"Did you plug the kettle in?"

"You have to plug it in?"

"Happy, I don't want coffee.
I want to sleep."

"Okay. Okay, John. You can sleep. Just
tell me ONE more story.
But not a scary one."

"One more story?"

"Yes. And I'll go to sleep.
I promise."

"Okay. Once upon a time . . ."

"WAIT! Are there any witches in this story?"

"No. No witches."

"Good. Okay. Continue."

". . . there were three little pigs and a big bad wolf . . ."

"A big bad wolf?"

"Yes."

"Try another story, John."

"Okay. Once upon a time, there were three bears . . ."

"Uhh . . . no, not that one."

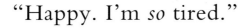

"Happy. I'm *so* tired."

"Just *one* more story, John. Please?"

"Okay. Once upon a time, there
was an ugly duckling."

"An ugly duckling?"

"Yes."

"And no witches
or
bad wolves
or
bears?"

"No. Just an ugly duckling, and some
other ducks, and some swans."

"Oh. That's a good story, John.
Tell me that one."

(And so he did.)

"Look, Happy. It's almost morning. Happy? . . . Happy?"

". . . Mmmmmmmmmmmm . . . 'night, John."

"Goodnight, Happy. Sleep tight.
Don't let the bed bugs bite."

"...Huh?...Did you say...*BED BUGS?*"

"Just kidding, Happy. There are no bed bugs.
Goodnight."

For every child who has ever thought of a mouse as a friend – P.R.

To Nav, who is patient and kind – A.T.B.

MOUSE TALES
Text Copyright © 2014 Philip Roy / Illustrations Copyright © 2014 Andrea Torrey Balsara
New and revised hard cover edition: May 2015

RONSDALE PRESS
3350 West 21st Avenue, Vancouver, B.C., Canada, V6S 1G7
www.ronsdalepress.com

Ronsdale Press wishes to thank the following for their support of its publishing program: the Canada Council for
the Arts, the Government of Canada through the Canada Book Fund, the British Columbia Arts Council and
the Province of British Columbia through the British Columbia Book Publishing Tax Credit program.

Library and Archives Canada Cataloguing in Publication

Roy, Philip, 1960–, author
Mouse tales / Philip Roy; Andrea Torrey Balsara, illustrator.

(Happy the pocket mouse)
ISBN 978-1-55380-444-4 (bound)

I. Balsara, Andrea Torrey, illustrator II. Title.

PS8635.O91144M68 2015   jC813'.6   C2015-902443-9

Printed on FSC paper in Canada by Friesens, Manitoba